2021 International Cultural Exchange Conference and 2021 International Environment Protection Awareness Conference

Editors of Proceedings:

Arianna Cao, Michelle Hua,
Allen Bryan, Zeru Peter Li

Ordering Information:

For orders and inquiries, please contact:
1-888-404-1388
www.goldtouchpress.com
book.orders@goldtouchpress.com

Printed in the United States of America

Table of Contents

Environmental Conference Student Speakers

Introduction

Hello everyone–participants, parents, and students! After several months of active preparation, the 2021 International Cultural Exchange and the International Environment Protection Awareness Conference was successfully held from 7/31/2021 to 8/1/2021. Congratulations to everyone for successfully completing the esteemed 2021 International Conference!

Totalling over 240 participants, the conference had speakers from more than 40 different cities in countries across the world, including the United States, China, Canada, Mexico, and Australia.

The 2021 Youth International Cultural Exchange Conference involves discussion of various cultures and their intertwining relationships. Our speakers spoke on topics from art to education. The conference is dedicated to improving global youth education and exchanges between different cultures. In addition to three keynote speakers, we also had a team of alumni from prestigious academic institutions who answered popular questions about the university application process and experience. We also had seven student speakers from different backgrounds, who discussed intriguing topics such as the art of moving and high school jazz.

The 2021 Youth International Environmental Protection Awareness Conference, a similar cultural exchange conference, contained an impressive lineup of guests, expert group members, and ten student speakers. They discussed environmentally friendly diets, air pollution, elephant protection, biodiversity loss, and much more.

We would also like to thank the participants for their dedication and our parents for their hard work and support, especially the parents of our students who organized this conference. Without everyone's efforts, we could not have had such a successful meeting. Thank you everyone!

Acknowledgments

We would like to thank all of our guest speakers for attending our conferences and providing us with such insightful speeches. We also thank our hosts for keeping the conference running smoothly, as well as the technology department for making sure the PowerPoint was functioning properly. Thank you to all the students who translated on stage, as well as those who transcribed and translated speeches for our proceedings.

Editors of Proceedings:

Arianna Cao, Michelle Hua, Allen Bryan, Zeru Peter Li

English to Chinese Translators and Interpreters:

Yi Zhang, Maggie Xu Li, Alice Yang, Zeru Peter Li

Proceedings Transcription:

Kevin Zhang, Owen Xu Li, Zeru Peter Li

Technical Support:

Zeru Peter Li

Hosts:

Allen Bryan, Alice Yang, Zeru Peter Li, Kevin Zhang, Owen Xu Li, Jack Wang

2021 International Cultural Exchange Conference

Location: Online | Date: July 31, 2021

This is the seventh annual International Cultural Exchange Conference. Our purpose is to exchange information and ideas about environmental issues and differences among cultures, ranging from the United States to China to Mexico, among professionals and students, as well as providing insight into education abroad. We have translated, transcribed, compiled, and edited the speeches of all our speakers.

Proceeding editors: Michelle Hua, Allen Bryan

Eric Williams

Eric Williams is the founder and creative director of the Silver Room, an innovative retail, arts, education and community events space opened in 1997. The Silver Room intersects the worlds of fashion, music and visual art, and acts as a boutique, gallery, and community arts center. Williams is committed to creating spaces and curating events that strengthen communities and fuel positive economic impact. He holds a degree in Finance from the University of Illinois at Chicago and is currently a Loeb Fellow at the Graduate school of Design at Harvard University.

African Americans' Contribution to the Arts During Uncertain Times

I wanted to talk about the contributions from African Americans to arts and culture from post-slavery time or during reconstruction to the present. I think it's really important to do that so we can understand how we got to where we are today. We all see the contributions of African Americans in American culture today, from singing to dancing, to what we see on TV and online. I wanted to make the connection to talk about the history of our contributions through the last two centuries.

So, you know when we were enslaved people in America, many of our cultures and our traditions were stopped, and they weren't allowed during the time of slavery. And, it was a secret thing in many ways that we had to sing and dance together, usually on Sundays, because the only day off was Sunday. So, we still figured out ways to communicate through music and dance on the plantation.

So if we fast forward a little bit, after reconstruction, this is an early photo from Congo Square in New Orleans, which speaks to one of the forms of music that we created, which was Jazz music, which was inspired from African music also. This is one of the earlier photos from the 1920s that speaks to Jazz. In New Orleans, before it went to New York City, before it migrated to Chicago, Memphis, Tennessee, it all started in New Orleans.

In many of the early recordings, many of the African American artists couldn't show their face on the cover of albums, many or all of them weren't allowed to perform, so they were forced to create their own communities. And, after New Orleans, the major city that we saw this emergence of arts and culture was in New York City, in Harlem. The Harlem Renaissance, which was the 1920s to the 1950s, was the intersection of music, of literature, of writers, of poets, of dance, of all kinds of arts and culture, in Harlem, which made it a very vibrant place to be, in the 1920s, 30s, 40s, and 50s. You can see the influence on American culture from the way they dressed, the fashion, also the poets, the writers, many famous writers from that time, they were all a part of this resurgence. In a time when African Americans still weren't allowed to have equal rights to other Americans, we were able to have this onslaught of energy of music and culture which really helped to shape a lot of other music that came later, be it Jazz music would be number one, but also Blues and American Rock music.

Here is a very famous photo from a place that I actually live now in Bronzeville, Chicago. These were some young boys who had just come home from church. And if you think about how they are dressed now, the suits, the ties, which was influenced by the Harlem Renaissance, were very elegant in the 30s and 40s. This photo became an iconic representation of what young African American people looked like. And this also speaks to the importance of Sunday and church, which is very important in African American culture, to present yourself in a certain manner. Even though the structural, the racism and everything else that was going on, the dignity these people had, and the way they presented themselves was very important.

As we move from the 30s and 40s to the 50s and 60s, another music emerged, which we know as American Rock n' Roll, which is important to know that that music came from African Americans, who started Rock n' Roll, which came from Jazz, which came from Blues, even Country and Western music. Unfortunately, a lot of black people weren't allowed to be on covers of albums and records, so you never actually saw the faces of many of these artists. Sometimes you would hear the music and they would have photos of white Americans on the cover, because they weren't allowed to show photos of African Americans on the cover. Many famous rock artists that you know of, like Elvis Presley and the Beatles, were directly influenced by black artists, Chuck Berry, Little Richard to name a couple

I want to fast forward to the 1960s, with the invention of Motown, which is a very important place in American music. The person who started Motown, his name was Berry Gordy from Detroit, so Detroit was known as the Motor city, so the "Mo" in "Motown". Berry Gordy tried to present a very elegant, classy, representation of what African Americans looked like in the 60s, again you see the suits and ties and a very beautiful example of what the culture looked like.

As we move on from the 60s, we go to the 70s. And a lot of music from the 70s, much of it was protest music, we always use music as a way to protest, societal bills, either speaking against a war, or racism, or injustice. So you start to see music really be more of a protest, and also at the same time you see us start to become these people who really wanted to express ourselves through dance, and the 70s was the time for that. There's a TV show called Soul Train that exemplifies a lot of that energy from the 70s. And you can see through these slides, that music and fashion were always intertwined. African Americans were always and still to this today are leaders in fashion, not just in America but all across the globe. The influence comes from our culture. You can see, you know, the big afros, and the clothes which influenced a lot of styles around the world.

As we moved from the 70s, mid 70s, late 70s, and early 80s, we came up big in Disco music and culture music. Again African Americans influenced the dance culture, from Studio 54, to what you see around the world now with electronic music. It all started from mostly black and gay clubs in New York City and in Chicago. That was the beginning of the dance music culture that we see around the world now.

Also in the 80s, the early 80s was the explosion of hip-hop and rap music. Mostly from New York City, on the east coast, a way to express ourselves through dance. Through music and dance, and also through rap, rap music and MCing. Again, much like earlier times in the 70s, in the 80s this was a response to what was going on in America and our culture, and dancing became a way to really express ourselves, and through hip-hop music you had four main pillars, the dance, which you see here, you had the rap, rap music, you had DJs, you had graffiti and arts. So it was a way to express yourself through music, through art, through dance. And that explosion in the early 80s still to this way was the beginning of hip-hop music which stemmed from African Americans and also from Puerto-Rican Americans. And also, I think what's important to know is that much of this music and this culture was started by young people. People in their teens, early twenties, and it was not meant to be mainstream, it was something that was really just for the people, and because it was so good, it became something that was mainstream. And a lot of these people didn't make any money when they started, they were just doing it because they loved it.

And I want to take a few steps forward to today, and I want to highlight one performer which everybody knows, Beyonce. A lot of performances are actually references to things I just spoke about, to African American culture, references to the 20s, to the 50s, to the Disco era. And it's interesting that someone like her is a worldwide phenomenon, a sensation, everybody knows her around the world, but a lot of her influence came from the history of African American culture.

This is a photo of my store, it's called the Silver Room. We've been open for 24 years. So, the space, it's a retail store, but it's really much more than that. It's a community gathering space. We have art openings, we have book signings, we have DJs in the store, we sell a lot of handmade merchandise, but the importance of this space is to bring people together through fashion and through music. And that's why for me, it's so important to present to you my influences throughout the last century from music and Jazz and fashion, that is a way to speak to people today, that this place can bring people together, in Chicago. We have so many issues that you might hear about in America in our society and in our cities when it comes to violence. It's important to have these kinds of spaces to bring people together.

So about 16 years ago, I started an event, it's a block party, it's a festival, as a way to bring our culture together. For me, it was influenced by, again, some of the things we talked about earlier, from Jazz music, to Blues music, to Disco, to house. As the way to have people celebrate, in Chicago. Many times, around the world in the media, you see very negative stereotypes of black people, of African Americans, and it's important that we show the positive side of us gathering, as well as having a good time and dancing. So we started this event 16 years ago, and last year we had 50,000 people come. And because of coronavirus, of course we didn't have it this year, or last year, but, next year.

So this is a slide of my newest business, my newest business venture, it's called Bronzeville Winery, Bronzeville is the neighborhood that I live in, a very important community in Chicago. It's a very beautiful restaurant. So again, for me, I want to think about ways we can bring people together, through fashion, through music, and now through food and wine. And I'm super excited, I'm very excited to have a place that we can gather and celebrate in our own community.

So, this is the last slide, but I wanted to leave you with an understanding of the contributions of African American culture in American culture and now worldwide culture. When we think about music, art, dance, and fashion, anything we think about comes from America, it comes from African Americans and our contributions. So, thank you again, I appreciate this opportunity.

Thank you all for participating in today's cultural exchange meeting. Take this opportunity to talk about some key elements in American culture.

Mr. Carl Scmidt

C arl Schmidt is a Business Education teacher at Monta Vista High School in Cupertino, California. He is one of the founders of Silicon Valley DECA, one of three California Districts. He just ended his second term as Chairperson of the California Association of DECA.

Mr. Schmidt completed his undergraduate work in Economics and later earned both a Masters of Business Administration (International Business) and a Master of Arts in Education (Educational Leadership). Before his teaching career, he was a senior consultant for Price Waterhouse in New York City and both a Manager, Information Systems, and Materials Manager for Xerox Corporation's Southern California Manufacturing Operations. He also had the opportunity to serve as a co-founder and Executive Vice President of a Global Electronics start-up.

Key Values of American Culture

The United States is very different from other countries in the world in that it is not composed of a single nation or race. The United States is a multi-ethnic melting pot, with people from all continents in Asia, Africa and Europe, and of course South America.

Summary of Discussion for today:

1. Cognitive Dissonance
2. Opportunity
3. Manifest Destiny
4. Mythology
5. The Business of America
6. Exceptionalism
7. Pluralism
8. Education
9. Creative Destruction

Cognitive dissonance

The definition of cognitive dissonance refers to the state of having inconsistent thoughts, beliefs, or attitudes, especially as relating to behavioral decisions and attitude change. So how should we understand? Cognitive dissonance refers to the presence of two or more opposing, contradictory, or conflicting views and ideas when it comes to behavioral decisions or attitude changes. For example, when the American people decided to take the initiative to overthrow the rule of the British Empire, we declared that "all men are created equal. Life, freedom, and the pursuit of happiness are the inalienable rights of everyone." However, when the Declaration of Independence was signed, many regions still reserved Slavery. Even during the War of Independence, we made many people who were persecuted for the overthrow of British rule into slavery with the patriots. There are countless examples of this.

We also have a concept that the individual is superior to the state, and the state is the creature of citizens. We also believe that the people have the right to abolish or overthrow any government, including our own government, as long as this government does not meet the needs of the people. We guarantee freedom of the press, freedom of religious belief, and freedom of assembly in the Constitution, and also stipulate how to legally own weapons. Just imagine, how can the people defend freedom of speech and challenge the government without having weapons?

F. Scott Fitzgerald once said: "The test of a first-rate intelligence is the ability to hold two opposing ideas in mind at the same time and still retain the ability to function."

Opportunity

What drives people to come to the United States? Going back to what we originally talked about, that is "opportunity." The factors that motivate people to leave their homes may be poverty, prejudice, power, etc., while the factors that attract people to the United States are respect for life and freedom; the possibility of pursuing happiness from scratch; the freedom of speech and belief, so that people can avoid fear. Furthermore, the United States has a large amount of land resources for people to produce and live.

Let's talk about the legacy of slavery.

At that time there were British, French and Spanish colonists on American soil. The War of Independence first began in the areas ruled by British colonists in the East of the United States.

1609: First permanent English settlement in Jamestown, Virginia

1619: First enslaved Africans brought by Portuguese to Jamestown and sold to English colonists

1688: First Anti-Slavery proclamation in the English Colonies of North America made by Francis Daniel Pastorius and his German-speaking Quakers/ Anabaptists in Germantown, Pennsylvania , based on the Golden Rule :" Do unto others as you would have them do unto you " (Matthew 7:12)

1776: " We hold these truths that all men are created equal ,that they are endowed by their Creator with certain unalienable rights, that among these are Life, Liberty, and the Pursuit of Happiness (Paragraph 2, Declaration of Independence)

1861: Confederate States of America established; Bombardment of Fort Sumter. United States War aims include Preservation of the Union and abolition of slavery

1863: Emancipation Proclamation Freeing Slaves in States in Rebellion 1865: The 13th Amendment forever abolished slavery

Manifest Destiny

Referring to a belief held by the United States in the nineteenth century. At that time, people believed that the United States was given the mandate to expand westward across the North American continent and reach the Pacific Ocean. The obstacle encountered across the North American continent is the French colony of Louisiana. There have been several wars between Britain and France in history. France has always intended to replace Britain and seize the position of European hegemony, but it has not been able to do so. Napoleon believed that the emerging United States of America would develop into the greatest threat to the British Empire, so he decided to sell Louisiana to the United States. In this way, the United States has completed the traverse from the Atlantic to the Pacific, and a large number of new European immigrants have poured into the Great Western Development.

The state of Texas in the United States is originally from Mexico. Mexico was once a Spanish colony. Before 1821, Texas was part of the Governor-General of New Spain. After Mexico became independent, due to the sparse population of Texans, the Mexican government invited Americans to emigrate, but there was a condition that they must intermarry with local Mexican women and convert to Roman Catholicism. At that time, many American immigrants acted like this. However, these immigrants are rebellious at heart and are unwilling to follow the Mexican government's regulations. In 1835, local immigrants in Texas began to organize and integrate and signed the first declaration in Goliad; in March 1836, Texas declared independence and established the Republic of Texas. In 1845, the United States announced that if the Republic of Texas was willing to join the United States, the United States would recognize the Golan River as its border. In the same year, Texas joined the United States. After that, Arizona, New Mexico, Utah, Nevada, and today the entire state of California were merged into the United States. The United States has become a vast country across the North American continent.

Horatio Alger Myth

Every country and nation has its legend. Behind the legend has a far-reaching influence on the thinking mode of various nationalities. The juvenile novel written by the famous American writer Horatio Alger is one of the most representative legends in American culture. The styles of stories told in his works are mostly consistent. Describe how poor young people struggle with adversity through honest hard work, a little luck and perseverance, and finally gain wealth and glory and realize the "American Dream".

"The Business of America is Business"

There used to be a president named Grover Cleveland, who was relatively reluctant to speak. A reporter once said to him, "Mr. President, I bet with my colleagues that you can say more than three words at a time." The president turned to him and said, "You lose (you lose only two words). But he did miss an important point is that one of the biggest differences between the United States and other countries lies in the American concept, that is, " The Business of America is Business." This statement was first put forward by former President Calvin Coolidge. Indeed, it has been the case to this day. Perhaps even more.

"American Exceptionalism"

That is, we believe that the United States is fundamentally different from other countries in the world. We don't have the long history of Asian, European, or Middle Eastern countries. We are a very young emerging country. From a Christian perspective, we are a "city upon a hill", advocating freedom and equality, individualism, republicanism, democracy, and laissez-faire and non-interventionist economic policies.

Pluralism

The United States is a country of immigrants. According to the laws of population push-pull migration, the early immigrants were generally one person in the family, possibly the father or the youngest son, who took root in the United States after hard work, and then took over the family one after another. "E pluribus unum" Latin, one of the mottos on the national emblem of the United States. People of various ethnic groups poured in from all over the world and merged their respective local cultures into a new culture-American culture.

This picture shows the racial statistics of American Ancestry 2000. Each color represents an ethnicity. You can see many colors in the picture. One of the light blue runs through things. What's interesting is that this color does not represent the British, but the German. Look at the pink and purple in the south, it's Hispanic. The deepest purple represents African descent. The light blue at the top represents French ancestry. The San Francisco generation gathers Chinese descent.

Britain and Germany are the two largest ethnic groups, but what is interesting is that there have been two major wars between the United States and them in history. What's more interesting is that most of the US military generals are of European descent. This shows how integrated American culture is.

Speaking of the Chinese community, Chinese immigrants to the United States are now the sixth generation. Chinese and American society are intertwined, closely linked and inseparable.

This is American society. People from all over the world come together not because of race or ethnicity, but because they recognize the same value-American values.

Education

We attach importance to education and insist that appropriate education should be provided to the public for free.

Societies reproduce themselves in only two ways, biologically and culturally. Education is the site of cultural reproduction."

John Dewey, a famous American educator and philosopher, once said, "What the best and wisest parent wants for his own child, that must the community want for all of its children."

Education has a profound impact on all aspects of social development. President Franklin Roosevelt once said: "Democracy cannot succeed unless those who express their choice are prepared to choose wisely. The real safeguard of democracy, therefore, is education."

Unless the people have the quality of implementation, there can be no democratic society and no democratic constitution. All this needs to be achieved through education.

The American education system is also diversified, including public, private, and private churches. All of this also guarantees the pluralistic nature of American society. If you don't like teachers in public schools, you can leave. If you can't change it, you can leave. If you can change it, you can change the school board or replace inappropriate teachers and staff. Public education system: What is the purpose of public education? It is to guarantee democracy. What is needed to guarantee democracy? Need to have the habit of critical thinking, creative thinking and lifelong learning. Teachers in public schools do not teach facts, but concepts. Instead of answering questions, they teach students how to ask and ask the right questions.

Creative Destruction

This concept is derived from capitalist writings. The incessant product and process innovation mechanism by which new production units replace outdated ones, is the essential fact about capitalism. The rise and fall of companies and industries have pushed the market in a more efficient direction.

No kind of technological power can last forever. There will always be other people, whether in the laboratory or in the garage, who will generate novel inspirations. We like this kind of destruction and look forward to this kind of destruction. For example, Edison's phonograph is one of the two most outstanding patents in his life. He set up a glorious company for this. But then new technologies continued to appear, a new type of phonograph replaced the old model, and a new company replaced the old company. Blockbuster, which used to be famous for renting video discs, was later replaced by Netflix, and Netflix will be replaced by other companies in the future; Facebook will replace the previous social software, and other emerging technologies will also replace Facebook in the future; Amazon replaces the previous Borders , The follow-up will definitely be replaced.

Critical Issues we are facing right now:

Coronavirus, Economic Recession
Technology, Innovation, Economic Disruption
Needed Job Skills and Immigration
Disconnect Demographic Changes
Health Care Education Climate Change

Finally, talking about the relationship between China and America, I would like to thank the Chinese people for providing America with the greatest gift of all: your people. Since their first arrival Chinese Americans have distinguished themselves in every sphere of life. Without them, America would be a lesser place. They are part of the American Tapestry, inseparable. Their legacy binds the two counties together forever.

Thank you all!

Jay H Jones, PhD

P rofessor Jones has a broad academic background, with concentrations in Botany, Microbiology, Chemistry, and Geology. His research and work experience includes Senior Research Geobotanist, researching oil and gas exploration (ARCO), Naturalist/Interpreter (National Park Service), Remote Sensing Consultant (NASA/Lockheed). He is currently in the field conducting floral surveys, as well as in the laboratory working with complex analytical instrumentation. As Professor of Biology and Biochemistry, Jones has taught an exceptionally broad range of courses including versions of an interdisciplinary course entitled: Toward a Sustainable Planet. Many of these courses have field components in which faculty and students see the global impact of the human species in various countries around the world.

Higher Education Should Be More Than You Expect!
(US Higher Education in the Post Covid-19 World)

Why do we go to higher education? Well, normally it's just to qualify for a job. I want to be an engineer. I want to be a physician, so that's the main reason that people go for a professional degree. One can make more money and have a more secure life and then also higher education gives you a certain level of prestige, putting you above other people who, perhaps, have not gone on for a higher degree. But college should provide more than just training for a job. It really needs to open your eyes, broaden your understanding of the world around you, and help you to become an informed global citizen. It needs to prepare you for a quality life, especially given the global challenge that we have. It needs to enhance your ability to contribute to the common good.

Most of all. Higher education today must help you understand and be able to meet the challenges of the new epic we are in the Anthropocene. Must [people] go to college with a specific profession in mind but 70% of students changed their mind before graduation. So you may go to college with a specific goal but chances are, you will change your goal during your education.

I loved biology and chemistry. So I went to college, thinking that Pharmacy would be my best career. So I started in a pre-pharmacy major. But when I got to college, I realized college was much more than just a training method for a profession. There were seminars, there was the Arts, there was music, there were visual arts. There were different types of talks and many different types of courses that were outside of my intended profession.

So very briefly, a college education is a broadening experience that teaches you more than just a career path.

When I went to school, I became a student research assistant. I got to know the faculty personally, I graduated two courses, shy of three Majors, and the general education courses that I had broadened me so that I could see a broad range of society and how our government, how social issues, how philosophy and arts, all fit together into a marvelous view of the world around me. I can see the world far better than before, and I no longer wanted to be a pharmacist. The pharmacy wasn't for me.

Well, I realize that I had a passion for research. I had a better understanding of the major areas of human knowledge and how they fit together for a deeper understanding of my own culture and traditions. I had an appreciation for the culture and traditions of others, and a better understanding of myself and my relationship to the universe.

For me, the college opened up the window so that I could see the world around me.

Higher education happens outside of the classrooms and laboratories; it happens in the university environment. This can be in the dormitories, in dining halls, public places, coffee houses. We're exposed to the thoughts and values of others. We are prompted to examine our own assumptions and traditions, the traditions and assumptions that we have grown up with in our own family. So very briefly higher education broadens your awareness of different perspectives and different ways of living.

There are many extracurricular activities. Including musical performances and art performances, Visual Arts has so many different things that you can explore and provide a much broader understanding and a richer understanding of the world around us. Make sure you take advantage of these activities. [And] stay connected with nature.

If you can go to a college that is near a natural area and not sequestered in an urban area. A place to getaway. When studying and so forth becomes demanding at times, it's very important to get away and to be in touch with the real world with nature.

General education consists of a broad range of courses that do not necessarily relate to your discipline. Why do we have to take these courses? They don't relate to my professional goal. But they're very important. The importance of general education is to help you to be an informed citizen. To better understand yourself and humanity and the universe, to develop critical-thinking skills, and to develop an appreciation for the arts and culture. It develops skills and knowledge for working with others and prepares you as the previous speaker has discussed for lifelong learning. This is only the beginning. Once you have the foundation, then you will continue learning throughout the rest of your life.

Values are interesting because they don't really relate to a specific discipline. We can learn knowledge and get the power of knowledge, but it is values that are critical in deciding what we do with that knowledge. Values determine what we do with knowledge. The power of the sciences, in particular, allows us to change things on a very large scale. But they can be used for good purposes, purposes that are constructive, or purposes that are destructive. Hopefully, as one goes through college, one will gain an appreciation for the need to have values that contribute to the common good.

Travel can be an important component as well. I have had the great fortune to be able to take students to many different countries around the world. Once you get into a different country, it changes your frame of view and it gives you a much better picture. Travel is very important if one can afford to do it.

These are some photographs from Costa Rica, which is one of the countries that I have taken as a student. It shows the production of coffee, something which I'm addicted to. But I understand that my consumption of coffee also has ecological implications by displacing the native vegetation. Travel allowed me to see this first hand.

Choosing a college or university is a very important step, and there are many factors that one has to take into account when choosing a different College. It depends on your goals. Some might want to hold a degree from a prestigious institution and this is the main goal. Some might want to go to a school that is specifically strong in engineering because they want to be an engineer.

Some might just go to a university to just learn and to answer the big questions in life. So it depends on what your goal is as to the type of college that you would choose.

There are many types of colleges and universities in the United States. We have community colleges, which are generally almost free and are free in some places. They provide training for different types of trades and preparation for transfer to a four-year college. They're inexpensive and students are self-motivated.

We have traditional four-year, undergraduate universities, and we have undergraduate universities with a master's degree program but no doctoral program and then we have what we call comprehensive doctoral-granting institutions. Which are classified into three categories, R1, R2, and R3, depending on how much emphasis they have on research. R1 has the most emphasis on research, R3 has the least.

Education is a secondary consideration. Select a college that fits your needs and desires. What is the best college to get? What am I looking for, how well prepared am I. You don't want to apply and be admitted to an institution, and then find out your preparation is inadequate.

How much individual attention will I need, and can I get it at this institution. At an R1 institution, you probably will not get much assistance. At a four-year school, especially the private four-year schools, you would get much more attention. Is the physical and cultural environment compatible with my needs and desires? [And] how much will it cost? All of these things are things that one would consider. State schools are generally less expensive. State schools tend to be large with less individual attention. Large State schools tend to have more activities and opportunities. Large privates offer a similar range of activities and opportunities but are more expensive. Small privates are generally expensive but provide more individual attention and greater concentration on values. The comprehensive doctoral-granting institutions R1 are highly research-centered. They're generally the best known with very good reputations. The reputation is based primarily on research and not on education. Finances often depend on grant overhead. Therefore, grants are often more important to the administration than the teaching and the tuition. The curriculum is often narrow and taught by non-tenure-track faculty.

The quality of undergraduate education, at least in the sciences is generally impacted. R2 and R3 doctor institutions usually provide better undergraduate education, research is still there, but there is a better balance between teaching and research. There are more opportunities for undergraduate research participation and however, the lower reputation does not hamper entrance into an R1 for a doctoral program. So for an undergraduate degree, R2 and R3 institutions are just fine.

However, I would provide some cautionary doses. That is, there are many institutions that are for-profit institutions, and the education that they provide is inadequate and expensive. Our former President Trump had a specific for-profit institution that was shown to be fragile and in terms of the products that it delivered. So be careful. Most of their budget goes to advertising and to the administration and the shareholders.

There's some transit education that is particularly disturbing even in the nonprofit sector. The bottom line has become more important, and some of the richness of education has suffered.

More attention is given today to resident centers, and dining options, and recreational facilities than Laboratories and art facilities.

SARS covid 2 effects. Well, here we are. So the current pandemic is causing higher education to have particular challenges. It has pushed us into the virtual world and unfortunately, it intensifies the effects of modification in most cases. Many administrators are seen this as a less expensive way to provide education. However, the difference between an isolated Zoom-based education and one that is emerging is really great and the serendipity and expected things you learned on campus cannot be replaced in the virtual environment. That does not mean that virtual tools are not important. It simply means that if we go that way, totally, we are going to be seriously compromised.

Virtual Labs. I have had to teach virtual biochemistry labs and they are horrible. We must keep the in-person face-to-face education.

Well, your education must prepare you for the challenges of the Anthropocene, the new epic that we are facing. As you can see the world is changing very, very rapidly. Most colleges and most curricula have not embraced the magnitude of the changes that we will be facing. I would ask that each one of you make sure that when you go to college that you seek out courses that will help you understand the magnitude of the changes we will face and also how to best deal with them to have a high-quality life.

Most schools have courses that you can take that will help you to prepare but you probably will have to actively seek those courses they have integrated into the curriculum in most majors, specifically business and many other disciplines.

Knowledge has been the most valuable thing in my life.

Thank you for the opportunity to chat with you, you're always welcome to get a hold of me.

The US College Panel — Q&A About U.S. Colleges

Panelists:

Albert Zeng is a graduate of Harvard University and moderates this panel discussion.

Kevin Bryan is a Sophomore at the University of Pennsylvania. He is Majoring in Neuroscience in the premed track. He currently does research for the Neuroscience department and the Colket Center, and is a reporter for the daily Pennsylvanian, as well as being involved with multiple clubs on campus.

Luis Perez is a senior software engineer at Facebook AI, helping to promote positive user content by teaching machines to understand text, image, and video. Previously, he was a senior research engineer at D-Mind where he reduced carbon emissions for vehicles by developing novel routing algorithms for google maps, and improved youtube's video recommendation through deep learning. He was a software engineer at Google working on large scale distributed systems and he received his BA cum laude in computer science from Harvard and a secondary in mathematics and a joint masters in artificial intelligence and theoretical computer science from Stanford.

Valerie Morales has 8 years of experience working with labor unions working in New York and Australia. During that time she has provided training and support for very successful campaigns. She has experience in providing direct help to members, as well as directing and organizing leadership to help improve data skills across their organizations. Her skills include assisting and interpretation of data analysis including data systems and supporting digital communications programs.

Ellen Zang is a senior strategic operations manager at Splunk. Spunk technology is designed to investigate, monitor, and analyze, and act on data at any scale. Previously she was executive director of "With Honor Action", where she worked with military veterans running for office and oversaw efforts to advocate for cross-partisan legislation. Earlier in her career, she was a deputy political director for the democratic senate campaign, and at the council for the US Senate Rules Committee. She received her BS in electrical engineering from Berkeley, and her Law Degree Cum Laude from Harvard.

What is the most important part of a college application?

Albert: It is hard to say what is the most important part of a college application, whether it is GPA or extracurriculars and the leadership experiences that come with extracurriculars. Your GPA is very critical. Without a top GPA, it is going to be very difficult to get into a top school. That said, there are many important aspects and you should not neglect any of them.

Luis: Yes, there are many factors. The way to think about it is what stage you are in the application process. In early high school it is important to get your fundamentals down. Be the best student you can and get the best grades you can and excel in academics. Once you get to the point of filling out the college application, especially for U. S. applications, the essays are very important. At that stage, essays are the things that you have the most control over and allow you to stand out from all the other applicants.

What age should students start preparing for college applications?

Luis: You should start preparing as early as possible. Don't do what I did and start preparing too late. I started thinking about it late in the sophomore year of high school. At that point, there is not much that you can change. At that time you have already spent two years of high school and if you have not been involved with clubs and organizations at that point, you have missed opportunities. So, I think you should begin as soon as you begin high school. You should have been thinking about what you wanted to do even before that.

Ellen: I agree with Luis. Preparing does not mean you cannot change, but you should think about your path.

Albert: To add onto that, the thing you want to avoid is getting into the junior year and applications are due in half a year and you are thinking, I don't have any extracurriculars and my grades are not that great, now what do I do to get into a good college. At that point it is a little bit late and there is not much you can do to really improve your chances except your essays. You don't want to be scrambling at that point looking for ways to stand out.

Kevin: I completely agree with the points that the others have made. Getting involved as a freshman is so important. There is still a lot of room for growth at that point and I would suggest getting involved in as many things as possible at that point. Being curious and exploring is very important. It will help you figure out what path to take in college when you get ready to apply for college. Also, keep a balance - stay healthy and happy, because mental health is also important.

What was your favorite part of the university you attended?

Albert: My favorite part was getting to meet so many types of people. I am from the Bay Area and people may act and think a certain way. College can bring together people of diverse backgrounds from many parts of the country.

Valarie: I went to UC Irvine, which has great weather all year round. Also, many of the professors I met actually wrote the books that we used, so we got to learn the material in depth. Also, while UC Irvine is great, it is also a starting point for many young faculty, who move on to other great universities. I was able to develop relationships with people who are now at many diverse places.

Kevin: One of the main attractions for me was to go to a school where the resources and opportunities abound. I am a neuroscience major, on the pre-med track and I wanted to join a lab. At the University of Pennsylvania, there are myriad labs to work in and you can usually find a lab that suits you. If you are a student that is ambitious and wants to work hard, there are many opportunities for you. One of the underrated aspects of Penn is its campus, which is integrated into the city of Philadelphia. Coming from a suburban environment, this was a great way to add to my experiences at college. Yet within the urban environment the campus is well defined, which is an aspect of Penn that I enjoy.

What are some things you did in high school that helped you get where you are?

Kevin: I did various things in high school and there is not one specific thing that got me to the college of my choice. I feel that as a neuroscience major I had to develop that science spike (demonstrated area of competence), by founding a science club and doing research. I also did other activities to develop well-roundedness. I was an athlete and captain of the crew team, which showed leadership. I wrote for a student magazine, which is now the basis for my work with the Daily Pennsylvanian, the student newspaper. I think it is cool that what I did in high school helped set the foundation of what I do in college. Make sure you enjoy what you do in high school, because you may be able to carry them over to college.

Valarie: I think you should read as much as possible in high school, including things you enjoy as well as things that will challenge your reading level. It is very valuable to be able to be a strong reader and to go through books quite quickly to get through college. It is a great skill to have once you are there.

Luis: Adding to what Kevin said, it is quite important to find the activities you are passionate about. Because if you enjoy them you have the incentive to make them better and to go out of your way to be a leader or President. Have your club go to different competitions, for example. This helps you shape the narrative of your high school experience and to develop strong relationships with people inside and outside of school who can serve as role models. That's what I did in high school that really helped.

That wraps up the panel portion of the conference. We hope you enjoyed it and got a new view of the American college experience.

Allen Bryan

I am a sophomore at Junipero Serra high school, an all-boys school in the Bay Area of California. I am interested in business and the sciences, and I am particularly interested in coursework that will help me pursue those fields. I hope to initiate a business and/or a pre-health club at my school. I also am interested in stock trading and hope to gain experience in that area. I enjoy playing piano for my school's amazing jazz ensemble. I also play football and run track for my school teams. Outside of school, I help raise funds for the underprivileged and I am an editor of a student run online magazine, Tempus.

Jazz in American High Schools

Jazz was born from the African American Communities in areas such as New Orleans, Chicago, and New York. These cities held some of the most diverse cultures in the USA, having influences of African, French. Pacific islanders, Europeans, and Native Americans all intertwined. Early jazz derived from West African music, influenced by the blues, ragtime, and French band music. At first jazz was mostly for dancing. (In later years, people would sit and listen to it.) After the first recordings of jazz were made in 1917, the music spread widely and developed rapidly. The evolution of jazz was led by a series of brilliant musicians such as Louis Armstrong, Duke Ellington, Charlie

Parker, and Miles Davis. Jazz developed into a series of different styles including traditional jazz, swing,bebop, cool jazz, and jazz rock, among others.

Jazz is considered one of the only forms of music developed in the United States. because of its diversity and inclusiveness. Jazz has all the elements of other music. It has melody; that's the tune of the song, the part you're most likely to remember. It has harmony, the notes that make the melody sound fuller. It has rhythm, which is the heartbeat of the song. But what sets jazz apart is its strong improvisational streak. That means making it up on the spot with no sheet music or structured memorization. There may not even be prior discussion with your bandmates. You just play and your discussion is on stage through the music. Improvisation is one of the most difficult aspects of Jazz to learn, but also the greatest once mastered. It usually comes in the form of a solo, allowing a single person to express themselves without having to play over the other musicians. Another great thing about this music is that it and its various styles is that it offers common ground between black and white, and other cultures, which is important in our divisive times.

Jazz has expanded beyond America to become a world artform, having found its way into most cosmopolitan cities. In America, jazz found its way out of New Orleans and into other major cities as jazz musicians traveled by the Mississippi river, by train, and road to cities like Chicago, New York, and Los Angeles. With this, new jazz variants developed all around the country: Chicago dominated night life with dance that engaged both white and black audiences. Harlem pianists developed the stride jazz variant, Kansas City developed swing, and New York musicians combined it with classical music instrumentation. Europeans were also big developers of Jazz, which had grown in popularity after World War II. What was so unique about Europe's variation of jazz was its influence from countries in Asia, the Middle East and

Africa. Soon, Jazz musicians from all over America were invited to play in Europe and jazz education and repertoire became more common. Jazz was also the music of the age in China in the 20s and 30s. It was enjoyed both by the upperclassmen as well as the farmers outside the major cities. Much of this musical expansion came from western imperialism during the Opium war. It spread through China in a style called Shidaiqu, which is a type of Chinese folk music and American jazz fusion started in Shanghai, when the English took control over that area.

While Jazz has seen a decline on the top charts of the music industry, influence is still strong. It has seen an explosive rise in schools across America. Jazz education has nearly quadrupled in the last 50 years, and it is unusual for a school not to have a jazz ensemble. Many schools perform at jazz competitions such as those hosted by the CMEA. Students now have unprecedented amounts of resources to better their understanding of Jazz. I myself play jazz in my school's jazz band and it is both challenging and tiring at times but when everyone comes together and you hear each instrument blend with the other, it is a beautiful thing.

Every day at school, I begin my day with jazz class before my other classes begin. There are many benefits that I have found from this. One is that it is a great energizer for your day. Another is that you learn to be a team player as well as developing your own identity as a musician. It is also a positive extracurricular for college applications with universities like Juilliard, Columbia, Johns Hopkins, and Northwestern having top jazz programs.

Alice Yang

Food Varieties

Today, I am really proud to be here as part of our conference to speak about "Food Variety".

I grew up in a traditional Chinese family, so I know a lot about Chinese food culture. Plus, my grandparents always tell me, "food has been part of our culture for thousands of years."

After I immigrated to the US, I discovered that there is a big difference in the way we prepare dishes, the table manners, and the food we eat. Therefore, through my personal experience, I'd like to focus on the cultural food differences between the Chinese and Americans.

In my opinion, American food culture can be categorized into 3 sections:

No.1 Efficiency and convenience. When I think of American food, I think about burgers, hotdogs, and pizzas. Also known as "fast food". And I think it represents the fast-paced lifestyle of the US.

No. 2 Self-service. When I went out with my American friends, I noticed that they only ordered their own dishes and preferred to eat individually, while sitting together. I didn't understand at first because, from what environment and culture I grew up in, we share food with one another all the time. But then I realized that this is how they express their politeness and respect toward each other.

No. 3 Long rectangular tables. At restaurants, the tables are often long and rectangular, which is convenient to sit side by side, especially at dinner parties. There is a certain distance between each person, and it's pretty easy for everyone to have small conversations. Kind of like a fellowship, the distance between each person isn't so intimate, but it's also not so distant either.

In my culture, it's pretty different. Chinese food focuses on balanced nutrition and nourishment for everyone, while pursuing perfection in color, aroma, and taste. For example, in summer, food can be chill, but not cold. Like what my grandma always tells me, you should only eat one ice cream per day on hot summer days, or the coldness will overwhelm your body. I think this shows that Chinese people are mellow, serene, and not so overpowering in many certain aspects, and determined to pursue the perfection of our wellbeing.

Secondly, Mutual Assistance Through food. We often help others to pick up food as an act of kindness, respect, and cherish ness toward that person, which is what my grandma always did for me, and I felt warm-hearted inside.

Thirdly, the Round table. During festivals, families and friends would all return home, and everyone would sit around a round table, chat and laugh while we enjoyed the delicious food that the adults prepared with utmost care. It was this round table full of laughter and joy that allowed us to bond closely with affection and respect towards our family and friends.

All in all, even though there are lots of differences between the two cultures, we are willing to respect each other's culture. Food is the bridge that connects us, either old or young, men and women, the relatives who passed away, and the ones who are still alive. Food reunites us; We sit together, share our food, and share our feelings during each other's holidays. Let's enjoy our different food, but at the same time, adapting to the differences in each other's cultures.

Peter Li

Peter Li is an incoming senior at Saratoga High School. He likes to read books, especially historical and mystery novels. Peter is a clarinet player in the Saratoga High School band, he enjoys his time in marching band. During his free time, he likes to play the clarinet, read books, and take photographs.

Blue Galaxy: Aiding the Effort in Stopping Covid-19

I will be presenting a business that my friends and I founded during the pandemic: Blue Galaxy.

First of all, what is this business? We are a group of Bay Area high school students that want to do something to help the effort in stopping the spread of COVID-19. Our business goal, as a company that manufactures personal protective equipment, is to put our most sincere effort into curbing the transmission rates of COVID-19 during the pandemic.

In the early stage of business planning, our team decided to design three types of protective coveralls and one type of face shield. Our principal designer, Rebecca Wu, contributed a lot to the brainstorming part. She drew tens of sketches for potential designs. Our advisor Jennifer Hao also made three-dimensional models for our face shields.

To put ideas in action, we first researched protective coverall standards around the world, especially the ones from the European Union, China (Guobiao), and the United States (CDC). We wanted to make sure that our coverall is effective at preventing pathogen transmission. Then, our team contacted companies in China that are experienced in manufacturing protective coveralls and gave them our designs and materials list.

We have three types of protective coveralls as shown below in these pictures. The first type of coverall is called waist zipper. Like its name, the waist zipper protective coverall has a zipper at its waist that makes it easier for those that prefer to wear it from the waist and the front. The second type that we designed and manufactured is called "side zipper". It goes from the left hand to the left shoulder. Essentially, wearers of this type enter the protective coverall from the side.

This would make it easier for people working at places with little to no space. Lastly, we have the front zipper, which has a zipper in front and under. It is pretty self-explanatory.

We went to several places, including clinics, hospitals, and dental care facilities. The photo on the left has our research assistant Allen Bryan donating protective coveralls. The other photo on this slide has Allen, Cindy, Alisa, and me donating protective coveralls and face shields to a dental care facility in Silicon Valley.

This is another dental care center we went to. And there's our designer Rebecca donating boxes of face shields and protective coveralls to another clinic. The photo on the right is Kevin Zhang donating to a dental office.

So, what are our current plans for the Summer and the Fall of 2021? We are currently working on version 2.0 of our face shields and contacting a new Chinese manufacturer to be a cooperator.

After production, we expect to list our face shields on Amazon for sale. Through this business, a lot of us learned about the mechanisms behind how a business functions. We also gained valuable insights into the production of medical protective coveralls and face shields. Thank you very much.

Jack Wang

Jack Wang is an incoming senior at Evergreen Valley High school. Jack's favorite subjects in school are Biology, Math, and Chemistry. He enjoys doing challenging math problems. He volunteers in a student run non-profit organization and teaches math classes to help the community of kids to reach their fullest potential. He likes to play basketball and competes in a variety of AAU tournaments. During his free time, he likes to play piano and chat with friends.

The Art of Moving

I would like to discuss the "Art of Moving."

How many times have you moved during the last 5 years?

Statistics study shows that moving is a very common thing in America where 10.1% of Americans move every year. Which means one out of 10 people has moved in a year. Move rate is very high. Just take myself as an example. Before I was 8 years old, I moved 4 times in 5 years in the USA, ranging from south east Alabama, to west coast California, then to midwest Ohio, back to west coast California, even moved again inside California.

Maybe I cannot say I am the most frequent mover, however, what I saw and experienced during these moves has shaped me how I am nowadays. I would like to share my feelings as a little boy then and my perspective as a young adult now.

Each move brings me new experiences and allows me to encounter different people and things in each area. First, people are very different. It can be the language they speak, their ethnicity, their culture, even their taste of music. With different people in different areas, the community is formed differently. The lifestyle in some areas could be very relaxed, while other areas could be very speedy. As a young boy, I had to learn how to adapt to each of these areas in order to fit in with the community. Now I would like to talk about 3 places I have lived and how they impacted my life.

Alabama, at least University of Alabama, is known for its amazing College Football program. And because the college football team is very successful, almost everyone in Alabama cares about football to a very high degree. The College Football Program has won 6 national championships in 15 years. Even when they didn't win the championship in a year, they were very close, say ranking #2 in the NCAA. While I was living in Alabama, watching football games and tailgating during football season were a must. Football brings thousands of people into usually quiet college town and also brings happy and relaxed family time. Alabama is also known for the book "To Kill A Mockingbird" and also for its Space Program in Huntsville, where the US Space and Rocket Center is located. It also has one of the largest zoos in America known as the Birmingham Zoo where it has over 500 animals. It is one of my favorite places to go.

Ohio is known for the Wright Brother who invented the airplane. Native Americans who lived there formed the Miami tribe, though I am not sure if this Miami tribe has any relation to the famous city in Florida. As a great fan of football I am, the Buckeyes, Ohio state university, plays strong in Football. Their mascot is from the official state tree – The Buckeyes.

California is not only known for Silicon Valley, where many worldwide high tech companies start from and headquarters are located, but also for many other things as well. For example, Hollywood, where many great movies were made and possibly one of the most visited areas in California. within Hollywood we have many tourist attractions such as Universal Studios where you can find many movie related attractions. In-N-Out is also a huge part of California culture because In-N-Out is very unique to California and most other states do not have this fast food chain so Californians take pride in how good the burger is compared to other common fast food giants such as Mcdonalds. In California there are many places where you can go sightseeing such as the Golden Gate Bridge in San Francisco.

What I describe could not cover all the differences from these areas. It is just a piece of the iceberg to show America is very diverse.

Earlier, the panel discussion talked about college, now I would like to talk about the important time before college, highschool Life. In Highschool, especially in America I feel that clubs are a significant part of your highschool life. By joining a club or many clubs, you have the opportunity to meet more people and make new friends. As shown in this picture this is my school's Chinese Club also known as the Chinese Student Union, but there are also many other clubs such as the math club, Key Club, Red Cross, etc… By joining a club you also could participate in many activities that the club will host and it's just a lot of fun to do.

I also want to talk about teachers because teachers are very important in the American school system as they write you recommendation letters and also determine your GPA. It is very important in America to try and get to know your teachers and let your teachers get to know you better, so that they can describe you more uniquely and completely when you ask for their recommendation letter to apply for a college.

There are also sports teams that you can participate in high school. I myself made the basketball team as a freshman, and there are other sports that you can try out for. And if you do make the team, you will have the chance to go to many tournaments to represent your school.

Besides Football games I already talked, , there is Thanksgiving that every American Celebrates. Previously I talked about cultures of specific areas. Thanksgiving is a holiday that everyone in America celebrates, and during this time we will eat turkey and be thankful for what we have, which is the tradition since the beginning of America. Of course, there are other holidays such as Christmas and 4th of July.

I believe this conference is a great platform to exchange life experience for students and parents from different countries and different areas. It is my pleasure to share my experience. Hopefully my experience may give you some perspective for American life. Thanks.

Aidan Cao

Turing your Kitchen into a Factory

At the beginning of every year, my community hosts a big Chinese New Year Festival. The 2020 Festival held at Evergreen Valley High School started with Chinese Drums and Kung Fu performances. Everyone was safe, happy and joyful until COVID hit. Of course, no one expected a deadly virus to start a pandemic, so this ceremony was probably one of the few big Chinese Ceremonies that year in Silicon Valley.

In February 2020, COVID started spreading in China, so many Chinese-Americans, including my parents, donated Personal Protective Equipment which includes face shields, medical masks, gloves, goggles, boots, and coveralls, to China.

In March 2020, the US COVID cases started to multiply. Doctors and nurses in America did not have enough protective equipment, so our robotics team wanted to help. Our team decided to use 3D printers, and I used a program called Fusion 360 to design ear savers, no-touch keys, and face shield frames. Our 3D printer was great since it had a large printing base, allowing you to print multiple objects at once. Our team sent samples of face shields to Santa Clara Valley Medical Center for feedback and we kept making revisions as we printed different models.

In April, the 3D printers were working non-stop other than at night. At this point, my kitchen had transformed into a face shield factory. My 3D printer was relatively new, so to keep it from wearing out too quickly, we calibrated the printing bed every so often to prevent printing errors.

A common problem for the medical workers who wear masks all day is that the band on the masks chafes the back of your ears. To solve that problem, I created ear-savers for the masks to hook onto instead of ears. We also made face shields that had 3 adjustable sizes. We assembled, packaged, and sent multiple boxes of equipment every week. This went on until the end of summer, helping over 20 hospitals, clinics, and medical centers. Some of the equipment was sent to the East Coast too, like to New York and Florida.

Our team was very proud that we could help the doctors and nurses. Every time I see the smiles on their faces, it makes me feel happy. We even received thank-you letters and cards from the medical workers. We also donated some equipment to several local schools. Later on, we improved our design for face shields and some of the designs are being considered for patents.

Through all of the hardships during the pandemic, my team and I learned to cooperate with others and help each other. No matter what problems we face in the future, we can always work together to overcome the difficulties.

Owen Xu Li

Owen was born and raised in Mexico. He studies at the American School Foundation in Mexico City as an incoming junior. Owen is very passionate about Environmental Sciences and hopes to pursue a career in this field. Owen has also performed in multiple musical plays and in his school's jazz ensemble.

Mexican Culture

I am a Chinese born in Mexico. My parents are authentic Chinese, born in China and came to Mexico in their twenties. They came here due to different reasons, however, in Mexico, they met each other, got to know each other, and fell in love with each other. They went back to China to get married and then decided to come back to Mexico. Therefore, my brother and I were born here.

Now more and more Chinese are coming and living here, but at that time there were not so many, and very few had their child born and grew up here. Due to the huge differences in language and eating habits, it is not easy for Chinese people to adapt to Mexican life. In addition, the educational concepts of Chinese and Mexicans are also very different, most Chinese in Mexico prefer to keep their children in China for education. My parents have hesitated after we were born, not knowing if they should let us go back to China. But my parents didn't like the idea of separating from us, so they decided to let us stay together in Mexico.

My brother and I started school at a very young age because my mom had to go to work. At that time we were the only Asian face in the school and got a lot of attention. The kids were very friendly, they came close to us to make friends. It took us only several months to be able to speak fluently in Spanish.

Now when I recall my early years in kindergarten, I am very grateful to the teachers and friends. It is your friendship and support that make us quickly integrate into the life of Mexico.

Food:

Many people ask me if I prefer Chinese food or Mexican food. It's hard for me to answer, since both of them are delicious and healthy. My mom usually prepares Chinese food at home, so I always go for Mexican food when I am outside.

The most well-known is the Taco, consisting of a tortilla filled with basically anything: if it fits in a tortilla, it's a taco. It is one of the most traditional Mexican foods, and there is anthropological evidence that the indigenous people living in the lake region of the Valley of Mexico traditionally ate tacos filled with small fish.

The most popular traditional breakfast dish in Mexico is Chilaquiles. It consists of lightly fried corn tortillas with red or green salsa, with fried eggs, chicken, cheese, and sour cream.

Guacamole is undoubtedly one of Mexico's most popular dishes, but few people know that this traditional sauce dates back to the time of the Aztecs. It is made from mashed-up avocados, onions, tomatoes, lemon juice, and chili peppers. Every time I eat tacos, I'll ask for guacamole as a side dish.

Another Aztec originated food is tamales. It was a traditional food for Mayan and Inca tribes who needed nourishing food on the go to take into battle. It is made from corn dough, wrapped in banana leaves or corn husks, stuffed with either a sweet or savory filling such as meats and cheese, fruits, vegetables, chilies, and mole.

People:

Mexican people like very much watching television, you'll notice that a typical Mexican home has a family room which is a television room, and apart from it, every bedroom has a television as well, even in a baby's bedroom. My mom always complains about how expensive books are in Mexico, maybe that's why people cannot afford to read books and prefer to watch television.

Mexican people are optimistic. They are not that worried like Asian people do, that's why you feel relaxed being with them. Many of my parents' Chinese friends who used to live in Mexico miss life in Mexico when they went back to China.

Mexican people are warm-hearted, willing to help, even when they are busy or don't know how they will still tend to give you a hand. However, this is a big one amongst many Mexicans and can bring some problems, in particular, if you get lost on the street and ask for directions. Rather than telling you they don't know, they'll instead provide a roundabout set of directions, together with a vague wave down the street, in what may or may not be the direction you need to go. So you always need to ask several people to get the right direction. If you take it positively, you'll understand they just don't like to let you down when you need a hand.

Children's Day:

Days before Children's Day, each generation, from 1 to 6 of primary, has been assigned to a task. I remember one year, my generation was assigned to be in charge of the disco room, which was our Taekwondo room, but we converted it into a disco room, where we partied for hours and hours. Another generation was in charge of the station of entertainment like the puzzle one, the haircut one, which was one of my favorites, I remember doing a haircut with my best friend Mario, a short-upwards-punk style haircut that we called the "Rhinoceros haircut".

A festival without food is not a festival, a few days before the celebration, the teacher will make a list of all kinds of foods, drinks, desserts, etc. so that everyone in the class will bring to share. If you raise your hand to bring a pizza, that's a promise for all, so you'd better keep your word and don't forget to bring it, otherwise, you'll have to eat alone, which is the saddest thing on that special day.

On Children's Day, the main focus is on the children and making them feel special. In shopping malls all over Mexico, special events with clowns, magicians, music, shows, and balloons take place. It is a festivity that is quite unique, full of laughter and play when adults are reminded of the importance of childhood and children teach us how joyful and simple life can be. That's why when I turned 12, I got very sad because that was the last time for me to enjoy Children's Day.

Day of the Dead:

Mexico has tremendous cultures and traditions, one of the most well-known is the Day of the Dead. Many people think it is a Mexican version of Halloween, which is quite logical because the dates are very close. However, it isn't. Halloween is a dark night of terror and mischief, although children are all dressed up funny and cute; the Day of the Dead is a unique Mexican festival that has its profound cultural background. The Pixar movie Coco interprets the meaning very well.

Day of the Dead originated several thousand years ago with the Aztecs, who considered mourning the dead disrespectful. That's why on the Day of the Dead, you don't see people crying or mourning, instead, they play music, sing, hold family parties, and offer delicious food to the dead family members' tombs. They think the dead are still members of the community, kept alive in memory and spirit, so long as the memory of love still exists.

The Food of the Dead is also full of legend. According to Mexican traditional belief, the dead work up a mighty hunger and thirst traveling from the spirit world back to the realm of the living, so some families place their dead loved one's favorite meal on the altar, and the offerings must be placed one night before, leaving a whole night for the dead to "eat", and the living family must eat up all the offerings early next morning, by this way, both the living and the dead are sharing the food as if they were together again.

The Day of the Dead is celebrated between October 31st and November 2nd. It is divided into two parts, one day is for commemorating the dead children, another day is for commemorating the dead adult.

Valentine's Day:

Valentine's Day in Mexico is known as Dia del Amor y la Amistad, which means the day of love and friendship. It is not all about romance, like most of the other countries do, but also for friends and families. Mexicans are big fans of a holiday, so it comes as no surprise that Valentine's Day is up there as one of Mexico's favorite festivities. You'll see balloon vendors with heart-shaped balloons, fresh flowers galore for sale on streets, and chocolates selling out at shops and convenience stores. It is true that celebrating this date has no connection with Mexican history, but then again: love is a cause for celebration for all human beings and civilizations.

One traditional Mexican celebration is that teenage boys and girls, in groups divided by sex, will walk past each other in a park while heading in opposite directions. If a boy likes one of the girls, he'll hand her a flower. If the girl is still holding the flower when they pass each other later, it means she likes him back.

Well, that sounds very romantic, in my school, we've never had such an activity, we usually have a gift exchange among classmates, we send roses to teachers, chocolates, and heart-shaped candy to loved friends, we also create hand-made cards for someone we think are special to us, and we'd love to show our affection towards them on this special day.

When I was in 5th grade, we had a very special celebration in school, which I realized later that it is not at all a newly invented celebration activity, but it was already there, and it was a very typical and unique event in the primary school in Mexico. The event is called Getting Married. A boy will invite a girl, or vice-versa, to go to a table where it says " Matrimonios " which means " Marriage " in Spanish, a teacher will sitting by that table as an official who gives the authorization of marriage. The teacher will ask both the boy and girl if they are agreed to get married, if the answer is YES, then the teacher will take out from the drawer a document and give it to the boy.

Birthday parties:

Mexican people are known for being warm, generous, and above all of these, festive. They are big fans of partying. And among the parties, a birthday party is probably the most common. When I was in lower school, I was invited to a birthday party every weekend.

Mexico has several unique birthday traditions. My favorite one is "la mordida," when the birthday girl or boy's hands are tied behind their back and their face is shoved into the cake for them to take the first bite, whilst everyone around them shouts " Mordida! Mordida! Mordida!" which means "taking a bite."

Mexico is one of the few Latin countries with a birthday song that's not simply a Spanish version of " Happy Birthday." Instead, Mexico has her own birthday song called Las Mañanitas, which means the Little Mornings. A song that describes the beauty of the morning in which the singer comes to congratulate the birthday boy or girl. One of my Spanish teachers told me that the song was only sung in the morning according to an old tradition, but nowadays it can be sung at any time of the day.

Piñata is a must-be for a birthday party, especially for the party of small kids. The Piñata is made out of hard paper and is decorated to look like a particularly festive object or animal, or a favorite cartoon role of the birthday boy or girl. It is painted with bright colors and filled with candies and small toys. Partygoers are blindfolded and take turns to hit it trying to break open the Piñata in order to enjoy the candies and toys. My brother and I were invited to countless birthday parties, but we never liked to hit the Piñata, I guess we were the only kids who disliked it. We had odd compassion towards the Piñata, feeling sorry to watch it being hit and torn open.

Arianna Cao

Why Mindset Matters More Than Physical Prowess in Sports

Training for the Olympics during a pandemic as a pregnant mother is no easy feat. The competitive environment in sports is ruthless enough–add the stress of losing your source of income due to sponsorship penalties for being pregnant–is it even possible? Yet, eleven-time Olympic medalist Allyson Felix, mother of two-year-old Camryn, won two more medals in Tokyo 2020. Just imagine the strength she possesses–and I don't only mean her muscular buildup.

Currently, attention in sports is centered on physical aspects–strength, speed, coordination. Little attention is given to the battle in the brain. "The constant grind," "never giving up," and other cliché terms fail to encompass the nuances of the competition mindset. Confidence, balancing sport and life, and managing emotions are not to be reduced to mere buzzwords.

As a competitive fencer myself, I've had crazy come-backs, lost due to fear, and learned the true meaning of the word "fight." On Independence Day, I competed in the annual Junior Olympics, placing bronze in the cadet division. But a few weeks earlier in the June North American Cup (NAC), I came in 83rd. How can there be such a drastic difference?

Confidence can make or break an athlete. In a competition, it is incredibly easy for an athlete's mind to be plagued by doubt or pessimism. Tensing up or hesitating are both clear signs that an athlete is too nervous to be playing their best. A more relaxed player is more likely to notice opportunities to score or adapt to the situation than one who is too busy fretting about irrelevant details.

During the downtime at the June NAC, my mind was preoccupied with school: AP tests, finals week, group presentations. When fencing, I was flustered. Every point my opponent scored took my confidence down a notch. I lost to a young 12-year-old, albeit a rather competent one, in the early rounds.

There are several aspects of confidence that should be examined: when performing skills, keeping up physical fitness, and learning new techniques. In a competition, there is no time to debate whether you should have slept earlier or gone to that extra practice. You've spent thousands of hours building up muscle memory, so trust your body—it knows what to do.

While practicing, a different form of confidence is required. Athletes constantly have to adapt, and this includes learning unfamiliar techniques, which involves making mistakes. Confidence is knowing that losses when practicing new skills don't determine your worth but are simply another step of the learning process. [insert personal]

Growth isn't linear. Some skills have steeper learning curves. While you might assume increased time and effort leads to more shiny medals and trophies, overtraining is detrimental. An athlete's worst nightmare is getting injuries that can put them out for months. In addition, overtraining can cause hormone imbalances and increased psychological stress, leading to depression, especially for student athletes.

Professional volleyball player, Victoria Garrick, explains her average schedule playing as a Division I athlete at UCSD: 6AM running, 16 units of class, 5 hour practice blocks, mandatory tutoring, office hours, studying for exams. There's barely any time to eat. Miss two days of school for a game out of state, makeup all the missing work, lather, rinse, repeat. It's no wonder how this led to situational depression, anxiety, and a binge-eating disorder. An athlete is human and requires time to recharge.

Taking a break when everyone else is practicing may seem contradictory to success. But when burnt out, Olympic-hopeful gymnast Katelyn Ohashi was relieved when she became too injured to continue competing. In college, she only rejoined the UCLA gymnastics team when her coach put "the human before the athlete" and encouraged her to "explore [her] passions outside of the sport." Reinvigorated, Ohashi finished as a 2018 NCAA Champion with 11 career perfect 10s.

Additionally, nobody is fearless. My coach always tells me that anybody who says they never get scared is lying. It's only a matter of who is able to take advantage of their nerves. Recently, after leading 14:10, I lost the fifteen point match. In the last moments, I had frozen, tensing up my muscles, unable to think or act. Meanwhile, the adrenaline pumping through my opponent had her moving faster with more accuracy. Emotions dictate our movements.

Nicole Ross, an Olympic fencer, once stated that at the highest levels, the game depends not so much on the physical skill level but more on who is mentally stronger.

During quarantine, we all did our duty and stayed in our houses. While athletes found creative ways to keep fit at home, many of us lost the competition mindset. As the world slowly acclimates to "normal" life, we athletes must be prepared to compete again. Believe in yourself, but don't push yourself past your limits and remember, everyone gets nervous. Cheers to Lee Kiefer for winning gold at the Tokyo Olympics in women's foil fencing!

Hello everyone, parents and students! After nearly a month of active preparations, I would like to congratulate everyone on completing this hard online/present activity.

Thanks to those who participated in the 2021 Youth International Cultural Exchange Conference. The meeting discussed various aspects of national culture and the relationship between them.

Our speakers discussed a wide range of topics from art to education. The conference is dedicated to improving global youth education and communication among different cultures.

The 2021 Youth International Environmental Protection Awareness Conference, a similar cultural exchange conference, had a lineup of outstanding guest and student speakers. They discussed a variety of topics, from environmentally friendly diets to air pollution, elephant protection, to the loss of Shenwu diversity.

This conference had over 150 participants from the United States, China, Canada, Mexico, and Australia, accumulating to over 40 cities.

We would also like to thank the parents for their hard work and support. Especially the parents of classmates organized by the venue. Without everyone's efforts, there would be no such successful meeting.

2021 Youth International Environmental Protection Awareness Conference

2021 Youth International Environment Protection Awareness Conference

Location: Online | Date: August 1, 2021

Interpreters for Guest Speakers: Zeru Peter Li, Yi Zhang

This has been the seventh annual Youth International Environment Protection Awareness Conference. The purpose is to have professionals and students exchange information and ideas about what we can do to help the environment. We have translated, transcribed, compiled, and edited the speeches of all our speakers.

Proceeding Editors: Arianna Cao, Peter Zeru Li

Dr. Jay Jones, PhD

Professor Jones has a broad academic background, with concentrations in Botany, Microbiology, Chemistry, and Geology. His research and work experience includes Senior Research Geobotanist, conducting research on oil and gas exploration (ARCO), Naturalist/Interpreter (National Park Service), Remote Sensing Consultant (NASA/Lockheed). He is currently in the field conducting floral surveys, as well as in the laboratory working with complex analytical instrumentation. As Professor of Biology and Biochemistry, Jones has taught an exceptionally broad range of courses including versions of an interdisciplinary course entitled: Toward a Sustainable Planet. Many of these courses have field components in which faculty and students see the global impact of the human species in various countries around the world.

Where Do We Go From Here?

We know we are facing real problems, we have wildfires, there are over 85 wildfires in the Western part of the United States burning right now. We have a global pandemic which we are all aware of, we have floods, we have droughts, we have more and more days above 100 degrees in our domain. About ⅓ of the days now in some parts of Arizona are above 100 Fahrenheit, [and] about 39 or 40 degrees Celsius. So we know we are facing problems, and the issue is where do we go from here? What can we do to live a quality life in this new geological epic?

We think about the Earth as an endless entity, but really, we live in a very thin layer on the surface of the Earth, probably around 2 to 3 miles in thickness. So it's less than the wax on an apple.

I divided the talk into 3 parts. The first part is the environmental problem. I am going to go over it very briefly because you are probably aware of this issue. The problem is this, the human population has outgrown the limited environment in which we live. When I checked on July 15th, there were 7.77 billion people on the surface of the Earth.

This is a satellite composite image put together that shows the human population on earth. Remember that even the area that does not have light still has a lot of people. It is just that they are not industrialized and they do not have much light. I like to think of the earth as being similar to a Petri dish as bacterial colonies. One of my majors was microbiology and what we would see is the colony will grow very slowly and faster and faster until they fill the whole plate and they die. That's scary.

This is a growth curve of bacteria, if you've studied biology you have probably seen this. But this also applies to other organisms as well. On this growth curve, we are positioned about right here, our population is starting to slow in terms of its growth but it's still growing very rapidly. We will probably add about half of the number of people right now before the middle of the century. We are going to add even more people to put a greater load on resources.

One of the reasons for this is the use of land and agriculture. What are the reasons for this? It's the use of land and agriculture is the primary use to which we put land. Agriculture is about 50% of the land area. Of that 77%, about three-quarters is for the production of livestock, meat, and dairy. And about 23% of the land is for crops that we consume directly. So, 77% of the land area is just for livestock in the food that they consume. Even though three-quarters of the land is in support of meat and dairy, only 18% or about one-fifth of our calories come from meat. Over 80%, that is about 4/5 comes from plant-based food, which is grown on this 23% of the landmass. We mistakenly believe that you have to eat meat or dairy to get protein, but that is not true. About two-thirds of the protein that we consume actually comes from plants.

This shows some of the uses and abuses, I should say, of land. Most of our natural habitat is gone. 97% of the tall grasslands of North America are gone. Because they're feeding cattle [and] cows to eat. These are confined animal operations. All of these areas that are being cultivated are to feed these animals. The animals that live here are gone, and the water becomes polluted.

We're deforesting the wooded areas. This is in Brazil and it shows rapid deforestation. This is in Madagascar. It's occurring around the world in the tropical rainforest. The Deltas and estuaries are no longer these spawning grounds for fish, etc. They're developed and they are put into agricultural use. This is Shanghai. This is the Nile Delta. This is a shrimp farm in India, that is on a Delta there. The estuaries are becoming confined to very limited areas of undeveloped estuaries. But this is the breeding ground for fish and they also are good for absorbing carbon dioxide: the greenhouse gases from the atmosphere. Not many left, 80% are gone. These are coastal habitats that are being used for aquaculture for growing shellfish and other organisms for our consumption.

That's the situation we're in.

Let's look at the consequences. This is part two.

The consequences are most of the wildlife and so forth is being squeezed out by our burgeoning population and Industrial Development. Two-thirds of the mammals of the world are gone. Half of the birds of the world are gone. Many species are going extinct. Even though the extinction rate may not impress people much, the fact that the number of individuals has deteriorated way below 50%, is very troublesome. Insect populations, for instance, have fallen dramatically. When insect populations fall, it means the birds don't have food to eat and therefore the bird populations fall as well.

This shows economic development and the fact that as economic development grows, the habitat and the number of wild species decreases. This destabilizes our environment and it is beginning to impact us. In the tropics alone, the rainforests alone, a hundred and thirty-five species are estimated to go extinct. Every day.

Fisheries depletion. Climate changes with floods, droughts, and wildfires. All of these things that we mentioned before, decrease in productivity and rising prices are inevitable. When the food productivity declines then the prices will increase. The cost of repairing the environment also is going to increase, when you pay more to repair things, you have less to meet the needs of people.

Many of our major cities are just a couple of meters above sea level and with sea-level rise, you get more flooding and more deterioration due to water. In the United States, this high water level has recently caused the collapse of the major apartment building. Many other buildings in Miami are also showing similar deterioration. Major drought. We're in the midst of a major drought in California. It is a historic drought. We have not experienced this before to this magnitude. Over 85 fires are burning in the western part of the United States, many hectares. Limited water means that cropland previously under cultivation is no longer supplied with water. This is an Almond Grove that has been deprived of water and of course, the trees die. When agriculture fails, the jobs of the people that work in the agriculture sector are also lost. We're losing agricultural productivity because of erosion and the accumulation of salts in soils, etc. As we limit the amount of agricultural acreage or hectares, we find that the price of food and so forth will increase more and more. Hurricanes are one of the consequences of climate change.

Pollution from the deepwater horizon. The spill was the biggest, but there are spills that occur around the world every day. The Fisheries especially, oysters and so forth, along the Gulf Coast are permanently damaged. They contain toxins, probably nuclear aromatic compounds, that are cancer-causing, even though people eat these if they are doing so, with some risk.

But it's important to remember that the environmental impact will not affect everyone equally. It depends on where you live. It depends on the wealth and resources that you have. It depends on the level of knowledge that you have and your profession. And it also depends on your level of self-sufficiency, knowing how to survive. A support network. Do you have people to depend on? It depends on governmental policies. Some people can be left out. Your age, and also random factors. You might just be in the path of a tornado.

It's important to understand that many have already been affected. The impact is not in the future for many. There are millions of ecological migrants around the world already because of crop failure, because of wars over limited resources. Because of rising temperatures and the inability to live in certain areas of the world. So it's important for us to understand that the impact is already here. It just depends on where you are and whether you personally are being affected.

The distribution of wealth in the world will have an impact on how many people can actually survive the challenges of the Anthropocene. In today's world, the rich are getting richer and the poor are staying static or getting worse. This shows global inequality in different aspects of well-being. Many people understand that this is really a social or moral issue, and it's interesting to note that there are many people that were in the Civil Rights Movement that are also now on the environmental movement to try to move us toward a more sustainable lifestyle. This is just an indication from almost a decade ago of the number of people that have been displaced by disasters, most of which are environmentally precipitated. So it's happening now, and it's been happening for quite some time.

Certain countries like the United States and China, and Europe to some degree impact the environment more than other countries. However, the suffering for these impacts is felt predominantly in other countries. So the countries that are least responsible tend to be the most affected by the actual impact of climate change.

The growing population causes us to put production into the agricultural land, which cannot be cultivated sustainably. In other words, we can grow crops for a while but they will not grow sustainably. When they're put into cultivation, the soil is gone. Ultimately, almost all of this soil is gone and one has nothing to do, but to perhaps have some goats and they can eat on the residual vegetation that would grow on this land. I've seen this in Mexico, in the state of Oaxaca.

One of the issues too, is that we are so isolated that we don't even see the changes that are occurring around us with nature. Most people don't even understand how their food is being raised. So if we are looking at the impact, we know that the environment is changing at an ever-increasing rate. We know it's largely driven by us and that the consequences of these changes cannot be accommodated with our current operating system. We must change our economic system and we must change our behavior to make it more sustainable.

Jennifer Hao PhD

D r. Hao holds a PhD from the University of California. She is a senior engineer in Silicon Valley and holds more than 30 US patents. Dr. Hao has a wide range of interests, likes writing and reading, and actively participates in social activities. Served as the coordinator of all volunteers for the San Francisco skating competition for three years. As the coordinator of Hearts for 10 years. Dr. Hao also won the international Toastmaster English speaking gold medal, leadership ability gold medal, and was awarded the first place in humorous speech. In the end, she successfully nurtured three outstanding children.

How You Can Live a Happier and Healthier Life During COVID-19

I want to thank Dr. Jones for his environment protection concepts and detailed plan on how to do it from his personal aspects. I learned a lot from his speech.

Coronavirus disease (COVID-19) was first reported from Wuhan, China, on 31 December 2019. Per wordometer, till this week there were more than 197 million people infected, 4.21 million people dead. For those recovered from Covid-19 infections a lot are still suffering.

As of today the World is in third covid-19 wave with uptrend numbers reporting due to rapidly spreaded covid-19 by delta variance. In the US, 49 states are seeing a surge in cases, and some experts say stricter vaccine mandates may be the best way to prevent a full downward spiral. President Biden announced new measures to boost vaccinations, including requiring that all federal employees must attest to being vaccinated or face strict protocols.

CDC New Guidance and Vaccination is fully vaccinated people need face masks indoors also. The good news are:

- Israel will begin offering a third shot of the Pfizer-BioNTech COVID-19 vaccine to people aged over 60 who have already been vaccinated, the country's prime minister announced on Thursday, becoming the first country to offer a third booster dose to its citizens.
- Pfizer data suggest third dose of Covid-19 vaccine 'strongly' boosts protection against Delta variant

Under Covid-19, everything seems different. No gym exercise, no coworker lunches together, no friends' parties.

Looking around, many people staying home are lonely without social opportunities and have difficulty purchasing living necessities.

The U.S. Census Bureau recently reported that a third of Americans show signs of clinical depression and anxiety. These and other mental conditions are becoming amplified during the recent pandemic, while COVID-19 patients and their families are also at high risk of developing depression and anxiety.

Experts predicted that Covid-19 and its variations will likely stay for 18 months to two years. How to live a life under Covid-19 is something we all need to learn. Here is what I am doing:

Be aware what is going on :

For example:

- Billionaires fly out of the space (7/11/21) (7/20/21)
- 2020 Olympic at Tokyo, Japan

- New changing CDC guidance
- Boris Johnson battle with umbrella

We could see a lot of fun things occurring around us. A lot of things you can enjoy, and a lot of things you can laugh…

Find alternative ways: Healthy activities and Exercise

In the past every morning I went to the gym, since the shelter-in-place order was issued, I have been unable to go to the gym. However, I increased my backyard planting capacities for self-grown vegetables and fruits as well as flowers. This not only provided my family with organic foods, but it also forced myself to exercise every day and reduced work stress so I felt happier.

Host Online Event in Real Time

Every summer we have a trip for events such as providing financial support to 55 underprivileged children in Pucheng, Shanxi, bringing books to left behind students, donating food and necessities to special needs children, and planting trees in Tibet.

It's easy to say that due to Covid-19, we can not do it. But we did it virtually and we made it!

1. Host International conferences virtually for two years
    a. 2020 and 2021 International Cultural Exchange Conference Focusing on Teens
    b. 2020/2021 Youth International Environmental Protection Awareness Conference
2. Virtual visit and financial supports 55/30 underprivileged students
3. Virtual visit and book supports left behind Children
4. Virtual visit and food supports special needs children in Xian, Shanxi
5. Fourth year plant trees in Tibet
6. Global Youth Leadership Design Entrepreneur Competition (GYLDE Competition)
7. International conference

<u>Connect with family and friends</u>

Family connected via Wechat…. To have fun….

1. The first news today 今日头条（掌上新闻 ）
   Singing across the Pacific, Cloud Chorus Concert of Global Chinese Family
   跨越太平洋的歌声，全球华夏儿女家庭云合唱音乐会
   http://toutiao.com/item/6844853269697659396/
   Singing across the Pacific, Cloud Chorus Concert of Global Chinese Family
   跨越太平洋的歌声，全球华夏儿女家庭云合唱音乐会

2. Today's headlines (news focus) 今日头条（新闻聚焦） Todayh'seadlines (news focus)
   跨越太平洋的歌声，全球华夏儿女家庭云合唱音乐会
   http://toutiao.com/item/6844852061998154243/

Environmental Panel

Speakers:

Albert Zeng is a Harvard graduate and will moderate this discussion.

Kevin Bryan is a Sophomore at the University of Pennsylvania. He is Majoring in Neuroscience in the premed track. He currently does research for the Neuroscience department and the Colket Center, and is a reporter for the daily Pennsylvanian, as well as being involved with multiple clubs on campus.

Luis Perez is a senior software engineer at Facebook AI, helping to promote positive user content by teaching machines to understand text, image, and video. Previously, he was a senior research engineer at D-Mind where he reduced carbon emissions for vehicles by developing novel routing algorithms for google maps, and improved youtube's video recommendation through deep learning. He was a software engineer at Google working on large scale distributed systems and he received his BA cum laude in computer science from Harvard and a secondary in mathematics and a joint masters in artificial intelligence and theoretical computer science from Stanford.

Valerie Morales has 8 years of experience working with labor unions working in New York and Australia. During that time she has provided training and support for very successful campaigns. She has experience in providing direct help to members, as well as directing and organizing leadership to help improve data skills across their organizations. Her skills include assisting and interpretation of data analysis including data systems and supporting digital communications programs.

Ellen Zang is a senior strategic operations manager at Splunk. Spunk technology is designed to investigate, monitor, and analyze, and act on data at any scale. Previously she was executive director of "With Honor Action", where she worked with military veterans running for office and oversaw efforts to advocate for cross-partisan legislation. Earlier in her career, she was a deputy political director for the democratic senate campaign, and at the council for the US Senate Rules Committee. She received her BS in electrical engineering from Berkeley, and her Law Degree Cum Laude from Harvard.

Environmental Issues

In your opinion, what is the biggest environmental issue we face today?

Kevin: While there are many significant issues we face today, one of the most critical is access to clean, fresh water. Many experts say that while we worry about fossil fuels and many non-renewable resources, in a few decades the major issue may be the lack of drinkable water and it is an important issue to consider.

Ellen: I agree with Kevin that there are many important issues. I would take the flip side of that and consider the importance of melting polar ice caps. Climate change is warming the arctic and increasing sea levels up to 3 mm annually. In the arctic, the Greenland ice sheet is melting and it is one of the bigger environmental issues of great concern. There are going to be places all around the world that used to be above the water and are now going to be below the water. This will cause not only environmental problems, but migration problems and geopolitical problems as places that have been populated for generations are no longer going to be habitable.

Are electric cars a good way to fight global climate change and are you going to get one?

Luis: I do think that electric vehicles are part of a solution to help create a cleaner energy grid across the world. Personally, I don't currently own an electric vehicle, but the next car I purchase will likely be a hybrid or an all-electric vehicle. Internal combustion vehicles produce a significant portion of greenhouse gasses and using electric vehicles will help us move pollution production toward single source, power generation. This will allow better management of the greenhouse gas output by letting us tackle the problem at that single source. This may allow us to migrate power production from coal and other fossil fuels to wind, solar, and other clean sources. This may even include nuclear power. I would say that it is a very complex problem, but my answer is yes for electric vehicles as part of the solution to climate change.

Ellen: Luis is spot on here and I do think that electric vehicles are a key part of helping to fight climate change. It has been positive to see companies like General Motors say that they will stop selling gasoline powered cars by 2035, pivoting to battery powered models. Volvo as well. It is interesting to see them build a business case for this. But, as Luis said, how the car is charged matters a lot. Also, battery recycling is also an important issue and may contribute to environmental issues. We should work to make them more recyclable and better for the environment. Also, I do not own an all electric vehicle, but do own a hybrid. I look forward to owning one as the technology improves.

What is your opinion on nuclear power as the solution to renewable energy.

Kevin: I think there are a variety of advantages and disadvantages to nuclear power that most people are familiar with. The broad answer is that as our technological ability to handle nuclear power on a larger scale improves, the use of nuclear power will increase and more people will become comfortable with it. One caveat is that nuclear power is not truly a renewable power source, since it depends on uranium which is mined. If uranium becomes limiting, then the costs will increase. Also, there is an environmental impact to mining uranium.

Will removing solar panels impact the environment?

Ellen: If they go into landfills, it will damage the environment. It should be a goal to make both their manufacture and disposal more environmentally friendly?

Luis: Yes, solar panels life spans are limited and advocating for increasing the lifespans or recycling the materials is critical. This also goes back to the nuclear power question and its environmental issues. I am personally a fan of nuclear power and think we should continue to explore that technology despite some of the risks. In order to have a sustainable power source, we will have to balance that across multiple power sources. One hundred percent of power cannot come from just wind, or just solar, or just nuclear, but a balance of those. Some new advances in nuclear power actually involve reprocessing spent waste from older nuclear power facilities. This will allow us to extract a higher percentage of energy from current materials and in a safer way. Overall, we should continue to ask these questions about what is to be done with the materials when their expected lifespan is over.

College Admissions

Albert: We are going to shift away from environmental issues to some questions that remained from yesterday's panel regarding the college application process.

What advice can you give to parents of elementary school children thinking long term about college application?

Kevin: The elementary school years are an important time to help children develop curiosity and good habits, such as being organized, goal oriented, and focused. Give them access to lots of different learning opportunities, so that when parents are not there, the children are still willing to learn.

Valarie: I would say it is important to be a part of organized sports where they can learn to work with a team, or even individual sports that allow them to develop a skill. This will help them release energy so that they will have the focus when it comes to school work. Even board games and card games allow them to develop strategic thinking skills and learn to work within the rules.

Is there anything that you would have done differently in high school to help you better prepare for college?

Kevin: Yes, I spoke a little about this yesterday. I think you should grab as many opportunities as possible in high school. You may feel a little uncomfortable joining clubs, and teams. I think high school is a time to figure out what you are really interested in and what you might want to pursue as a career. I definitely regret not pursuing more of these opportunities. I tried to do a better job in college by coming into a new environment and trying new things – things I would not have necessarily done before. So, definitely get out of your comfort zone and do something new. It may even help you in your college application.

Ellen attended both UC Berkeley and Harvard. What did you find were the differences between top public and private universities?.

Ellen: I think there are major differences and they have tradeoffs. At Harvard Law school, I saw that there was a lot of help that Harvard undergrads received in terms of advising, guidance in writing essays, writing letters of recommendation, etc. When I was an undergrad at Berkeley, in the school of engineering, it definitely felt like there was less guidance. It was more of a struggle to figure out the law school application process on my own. On the other hand, I felt having to do this on my own helped make me more resilient and I feel that I am more resourceful in my life because I had to do that on my own and did not have the guidance that the private institution provided. The other side is the wealth of opportunities that a school like Harvard provides. If you want to do something, you could usually find a professor to sponsor you. For example, I spent several semesters studying in China, where most public schools may not provide the resources I needed.

Albert: I think that is all we have time for in the panel. Thanks to the Zoom audience for so many interesting questions and thanks to our panelists for insightful answers.

Kevin Zhang

Kevin Zhang is a rising 11th grader who attends Mountain View High School in Mountain View, California. He enjoys computers, science, math, and learning new things.

Air Pollution

Hello everybody, my name is Kevin Zhang, and I will be talking about Air Pollution.

So, what is air pollution? Air pollution is harmful solid particles and gas in the air. Chemicals from factories, car emissions, dust, pollen, and ozone can all be what makes up air pollution.

Particulate matter refers to harmful particles in the air. The particulate matter scale is used to measure the size of particles in the air. The smaller the particles are, the more potentially dangerous they are. PM2.5 particles, which are particles less than 2.5 microns in diameter, can easily reach deep into the human body and cause severe damage to the heart and lungs. The Air Quality Index, or AQI, is widely used to measure the amount of pollution in the air and the danger level of outdoor activity.

So, how can air pollution impact human health? Air pollution is tied to 6 million deaths annually around the world, an estimated 1 million of which are Chinese. Coarse harmful particles in the air can penetrate the upper respiratory system, and finer particles can penetrate even deeper into the body. Exposure to air pollution can cause eye and nose irritation, respiratory diseases, and heart disease, and also aggravate existing respiratory and heart conditions. Further prolonged exposure to serious air pollution can lead to severe conditions such as Alzheimer's disease, birth defects, and cancer.

Polluted air can cause many forms of damage to the surrounding environment. Eutrophication, or excessive amounts of nutrients in natural bodies of water, can be caused by polluted runoff or rain. Dense plant growth can then occur and block out sunlight and soak up vital nutrients, causing animal death. Acid rain, or rain mixed with chemicals and pollution, can destroy habitats and crops. Air pollution can wear away at the ozone layer, which protects the earth from ultraviolet light. Climate change can occur from gas trapped beneath the atmosphere of the earth.

However, you can still help with this issue. Reducing car trips, and instead walking, biking, or using public transportation will reduce the car emissions you contribute to. Getting smog checks and maintaining car engines will make sure your car won't be excessively emitting. Tires can sometimes contain gases harmful to the environment. Fixing leaking tires will prevent the tires from releasing harmful gas into the environment. Reducing use of wood stoves and fireplaces will reduce the amount of gas and smoke that goes into the air. Make sure to save energy whenever possible and buy energy-efficient products. Quitting smoking or restraining yourself from smoking indoors or where smoking is prohibited will greatly benefit public and indoor air quality.

Thanks for listening, everyone!

Alice Yang

Alice Yang is an incoming Biology major sophomore at Diablo Valley College. She loves to improve herself and challenge herself through all kinds of ways. Besides studying, in her leisure time, she loves to read crime and detective books to gain knowledge on criminal psychology. She felt fulfilled by using her time wisely everyday!

Solids Waste in Water is Threatening Marine Organisms and Plants

Good evening or good morning, my name is Alice. My speech, titled, "Solids Waste in Water is Threatening our Marine organisms and Plants."

The specific waste I'd like to discuss is plastic.

According to the United Nations Environment Programme (UNEP), we are producing about 300 million tons of plastic waste per year.

Plastic waste has two main problems, the first one is water pollution to our marine organisms.

According to the Condor Ferries webpage, "Marine & Ocean Pollution Statistics & Facts 2020-2021", about 100,000 oceanic lives die annually, just from the number of plastic wastes dumped into the ocean. Just North Pacific fish alone ingest about 12-14,000 tons of plastic yearly, while ⅓ of these marine creatures are entangled in plastic litter. The researchers also stated that "500 marine locations are now recorded as dead zones globally, currently the size of the United Kingdom's surface (245,000 km²)."

As a matter of fact, this problem is also threatening humans. As the webpage has mentioned, most of the fish or marine life we consume would have consumed plastic, which means we are also consuming toxic plastic. The plastic may contain lead, mercury, or other heavy metals that are widely known to cause health problems.

The second problem is soil pollution, which can also be considered as the problem of non-degradable or non-recyclable.

"500 MILLION plastic straws are used EVERY DAY in America. That's enough to circle the Earth twice," was reported by National Geographic's author Laura Parker. Nearly all of these plastics aren't recycled. "Plastic takes more than 400 years to degrade, so most of it still exists in some form." 79% of the 6.3 billion metric tons of plastic waste that are concentrated in landfills are spreading into the natural environment. If this continues, every millimeter of land which we humans and plants depend on will become a plastic landfill. Plants will not grow, humans and other land organisms will be on the verge of extinction. So we must act.

We need to solve this problem at its origin. The best resolution is to reduce the usage of plastic. Bottled water contains microplastics, harmful chemicals like phthalate, and a type of parasite known as cryptosporidium. As CDC points out in its website, "Drinking Water: Commercially Bottled Water", "The parasite Cryptosporidium can cause chronic or severe illness and even life-threatening symptoms in people with weakened immune systems. Healthy people would be more likely to develop a mild illness from this parasite." So not only is the plastic bottle harmful to the environment, the contaminated water is actually quite harmful to us consumers. Not to mention the marine organisms and plants.

It is us who produced plastic, and also it is us who cause plastic pollution, and now our waste is threatening our community.

Therefore, let's reduce the use of plastic to protect the environment and all living organisms living in it, such as ourselves, our marine animals, and plants.

Matthew Li

Matthew Li is an incoming freshman at Gulliver Prep. He likes to play chess and games.

Deforestation

Deforestation refers to the decrease in forest areas across the world that is used for other purposes such as agriculture, urbanization, cattle ranching, or mining. Over the decade since 2010, the net loss in forests globally was 4.7 million hectares per year. The UN FAO estimates that 10 million hectares of forest were cut down each year. Around half of this deforestation is offset by regrowing forests, About 30% of Earth's land surface is covered by forests. Overall we lose around five million hectares of forest each year.

Some causes of deforestation are Wildfires, Agricultural expansion, Wood extraction, Construction Mining, Cattle ranching.

Cattle ranching: Mongabay states that "the majority deforestation in the Amazon Basin since the 1960s has been caused by cattle ranchers and land speculators who burned huge tracts of rainforest for pasture." Additionally, "cattle are a low-risk investment relative to cash crops which are more subject to wild price swings and pest infestations."

Mining: Mongabay reports that "Large-scale mining operations, especially those using open-pit mining techniques, can result in significant deforestation through forest clearing and the construction of roads which open remote forest areas to transient settlers, land speculators, and small-scale miners." An analysis by the World Bank suggests that 44% of all operational mines lie in forests. This represents 1,539 mines, with another 1,826 in development or currently inactive. Mining activities have driven 7% of deforestation, according to a 2012 assessment.

Nigeria: Trees used to cover approximately 50% of the land in this country. According to the FAO (Food and Agriculture Organization), Nigeria has the world's highest deforestation rate of primary forests. It has lost more than half of its primary forest in the last five years.

Brazil: Cattle ranching and agriculture is the leading cause of deforestation in the Amazon rainforest. Mongabay states, "In Brazil, this has been the case since at least the 1970s: Today the figure in Brazil is closer to 70 percent." As in Brazil farmers are purposefully burning down the Amazon rainforest for more space for farming. The Bemidji Pioneer reports that "Farmers have long used fire to cut through jungle too dense for machines. The burned vegetation makes the soil fertile and cuts down on pests. But fire also plays a key role in illegal deforestation."

America: The United States Deforestation Rates & Statistics states that "the main causes of deforestation in America are agricultural expansion, wood extraction and wildfires (e.g., logging or wood harvest for domestic fuel or charcoal), and infrastructure expansion such as road building and urbanization." Global Forest Watch says that "In 2010, the United States had 252Mha(Million hectare meter) of natural forest, extending over 29% of its land area. In 2020, it lost 1.59Mha of natural forest, equivalent to 683Mt(Megatonne) of CO_2 of emissions."

We need to stop deforestation because the forest is home to many rare species. National Geographic informs us that "80% of earth's terrestrial animals and plants live in forests. By destroying the forests, the natural habitats of terrestrial animals are destroyed including the orangutan, Sumatran tiger, and many species of birds." A study by Olofin Emmanuel shows that "the removal of trees without sufficient reforestation has resulted in habitat damage, soil erosion, biodiversity loss, and aridity."

Deforestation is a cause of global warming and climate change because forestry and agriculture is responsible for 24% of global greenhouse gas emissions. Forests trap carbon and help stabilize the world's climate. When forests are trashed, the carbon trapped in trees, their roots and the soil is released into the atmosphere. Deforestation increased greenhouse gases in the atmosphere, deforestation accounts for up to 20% of all carbon emissions.

Some ways to solve this are reforestation, reducing the use of paper, and recycling paper.

Deforestation is solved by reforestation. According to MintCoinFund, "Recovering forest restores habitat loss and degradation and threats to species health."

Reduce consumption of paper. HS Business states that "reducing your usage of paper helps to prevent trees from being cut down and eliminates the energy that is used to convert a tree into a piece of white printing paper. Using less paper also helps you to reduce the amount of waste you have."

Recycling paper. As paper is made from wood, recycling it conserves trees and other natural resources, saves energy and reduces greenhouse gases that are emitted through. Logging is one of the biggest sources of steady deforestation. Recycling paper decreases the need for logging by paper making industries.

Nathaniel Guo

Nathaniel Guo is an incoming freshman at Irvington High. He likes to play video games such as Minecraft, Tetris, and Tf2. He has an interest in science and philosophy. In his free time he likes sharpening his skills in tetris.

Santony Duan

Santony Duan is a rising freshman at Irvington High School. He enjoys playing games and spending time with his friends such as Nathaniel. He also likes to play basketball and spend time outdoors.

Chiakuang (Roger) Tan

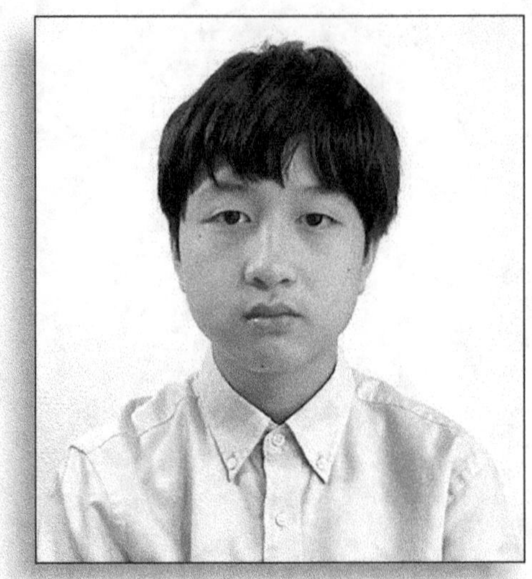

R oger is a rising freshman in Mission San Jose High School. He is a gamer and is interested in mathematics and physics. He mainly focuses on getting better at his worst subject, history.

Loss of Biodiversity

What is biodiversity? Biodiversity is the variety of life in the world. The more species there are, the more diversity there is in the world. However, we are losing more and more species each year, and this is a huge problem, because biodiversity is quite important, as every ecosystem relies on a variety of species to work and maintain balance.

It is very important to stop the loss of biodiversity since the deprivation of one species in an ecosystem will influence other species in the same food chain to change in population up and down, which would lead to potentially catastrophic effects. For instance, suppose that people started killing lions, the result would be a mass increase in antelopes, which will cause more grazing and less grass, which affects other animals that eat grass. The lack of biodiversity in an ecosystem will disturb the balance of that ecosystem, since even with one species gone, the structure of that ecosystem will disappear. For example, in an ecosystem without trees, many animals would die out, due to poor air quality control, and no food being provided to the creatures that depend on these trees for food. Not only that, but it is theorized that as microbes in an ecosystem die out, our immune systems become weaker, due to them not being exposed to beneficial microbes.

How can we solve this constantly growing problem? There are multiple ways to fix this ever growing issue. We can be careful and responsible when travelling in order to avoid importing invasive species that may have negative impacts on the environment. A major reason why we are losing more unique species is due to invasive species that actively or passively harm other species. Which in turn will likely cause them to start dying and possibly even go extinct.

We can recycle and compost certain items in order to reduce waste and stop pollution which in turn helps stop biodiversity loss, since millions of animals are affected and harmed by pollution per year due to insufficient trash management and recycling. Recycling and composting will not only help stop loss of biodiversity, it also helps the planet as a whole, since less pollution means better living conditions. We can also use fewer fossil fuels and gas-powered cars, which will prevent air pollution and improve the conditions of habitats necessary for living things to survive.

In conclusion, it is crucial that we resolve the loss of biodiversity. If we ignore this problem and continue like we are right now, we'll soon only have a few unique species left in this world. We must do a lot in order to conserve the diverse amount of organisms in this world.

Allen Bryan

I am a sophomore at Junipero Serra high school, an all boys school in California. I am interested in biomedical research, health sciences and in business. I am hoping to create the school's first DECA business club. I am also interested in stock trading, as well as how stocks help to fund business. I enjoy playing piano for my school's jazz band and enjoy improving my skills in that area. I also play football and run track for my high school. Outside of school, I am an editor for an online magazine and work as a Vice-President for HEARTS non-profit.

New Ideas for Clean Water

The World Health Organization says that at least 2 billion people in the world depend on drinking water sources that have been contaminated by fecal material. This is linked to transmission of diseases such as cholera, typhoid, and dysentery. I wondered why doesn't everyone have clean water.

Providing clean water can be a very expensive and sophisticated process requiring a large amount of energy. In the U.S., we devote 5-6% of our electric output to our water infrastructure.

With over 7 billion people on Earth and our economic systems based upon expanding populations, the need for better management of our energy resources, as well as the increasing amounts of human waste products will be an ever growing challenge. The process of treating wastewater in America is a huge burden in terms of infrastructure and electricity used.Reducing the cost of powering the wastewater treatment infrastructure is very challenging. But, scientists have found that there is unutilized energy in the organic material in the waste water itself. If fully utilized that is about 4-10 times the power needed for the treatment process.

A microbial fuel cell is a device in which microorganisms degrade complex organic materials to produce an electric current. The process is typically carried out by building a two chambered system. The anaerobic (no oxygen) chamber contains: microorganisms, an anode, and organic material upon which the microorganisms feed. The microorganisms form a film over the anode and send electrons, which traverse a wire to an aerobic (oxygenated) cathode chamber. The H+ (hydrogen ions) take an alternate path through a semipermeable membrane. The electric current flowing between the chambers can be used to do work. The goal is to have this integrated into the wastewater treatment plant to reduce the power costs of water treatment by producing the power onsite.

Removing pathogenic organisms is another process in wastewater treatment that can be improved. In most cases chlorine is used as the most effective way to kill these disease causing organisms, but removal of this chemical from the effluent is sometimes difficult. The chlorine is considered to be very damaging to the environment. There is often a high cost to removing chlorine from the effluent. A new solution to the problem is using peracetic acid. Peracetic acid is what is used to sanitize fruits and vegetables for the local supermarket. It breaks down to acetic acid, water, and oxygen, all of which are safe for the environment. The cost for peracetic acid was originally high, but has come down as more and more waste treatment plants adopt it and economies of scale come into play.

A third great idea for improving access to clean water is an ingenious invention called the Janicki Omni Processor. It was developed with the help of the Gates Foundation. This device improves the lives of people living in areas with little to no waste water management by taking in solid and liquid waste, burning the solid waste, and producing drinkable water from the liquid. It is an apparatus that is very effective for areas without large scale waste treatment systems, and may in some cases, be less expensive to deploy than large scale water treatment.

Thank you so much for listening to me and everyone else who spoke today. Remember that the world population is growing, and freshwater is growing scarce. We need to find new ways to manage our resources. But remember, our simplest method may be to conserve by making good choices.